A

Atmosp

MW01711585

The air that surrounds us

B Biodiversity

The variety of life that can
be found on earth

C Carbon Footprint

A measure of carbon dioxide
produced by human activities

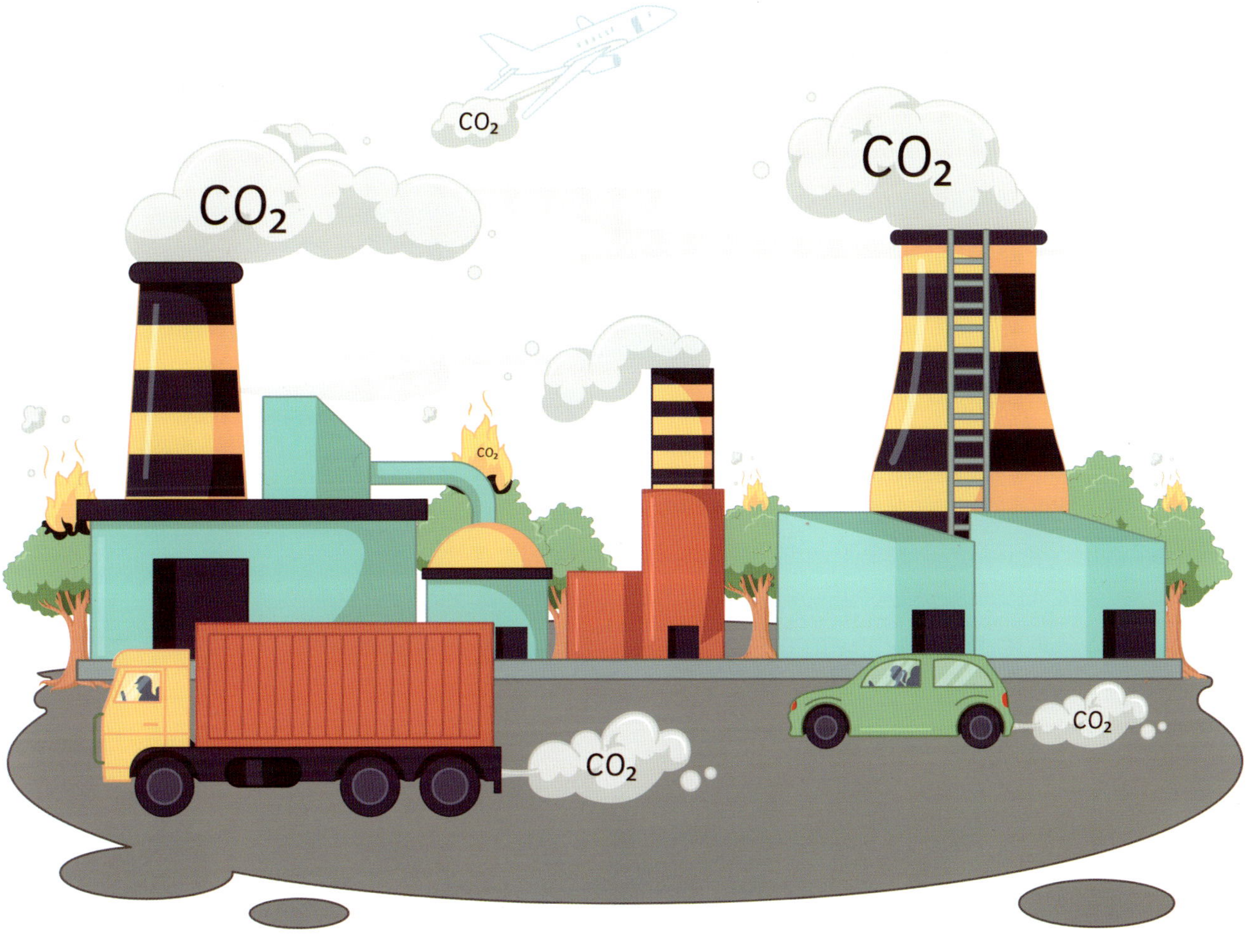

D Deforestation

Cutting down of trees

E Environment

Anything that surrounds us

F Flora and Fauna

Plants and Animals

G Global Warming

An increase in the earth's temperature caused by human activities

H Habitat

A place where animals and plants live

I

Incinerator

A machine used to burn waste

J

Jungle

A forest with dense
trees, plants and animals

K Keystone Species

A living thing that other plants and animals depend on

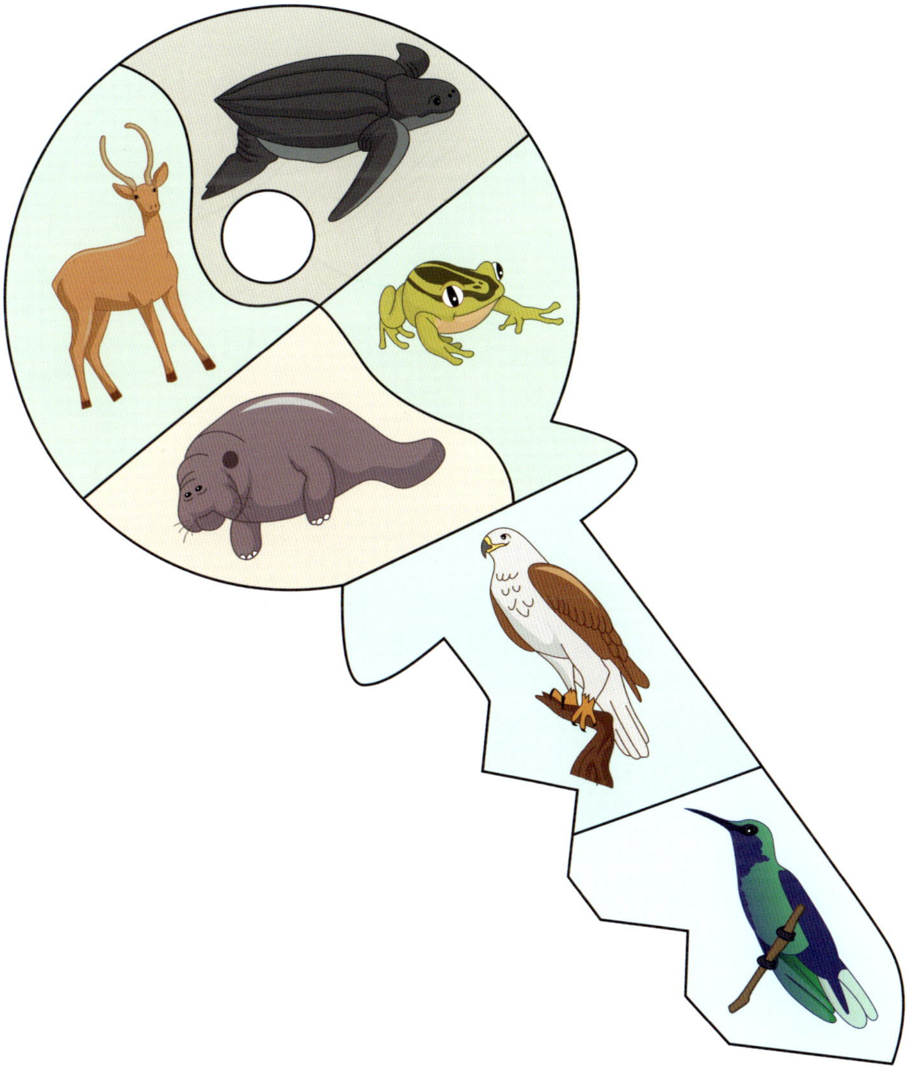

L

Landfill

A place where
waste is stored

M

Mangroves

A group of trees and shrubs
that grow in coastal areas

N

Noise

Unwanted sound

O

Ozone Layer

A thin protective layer of gas that protects us from harmful sun rays

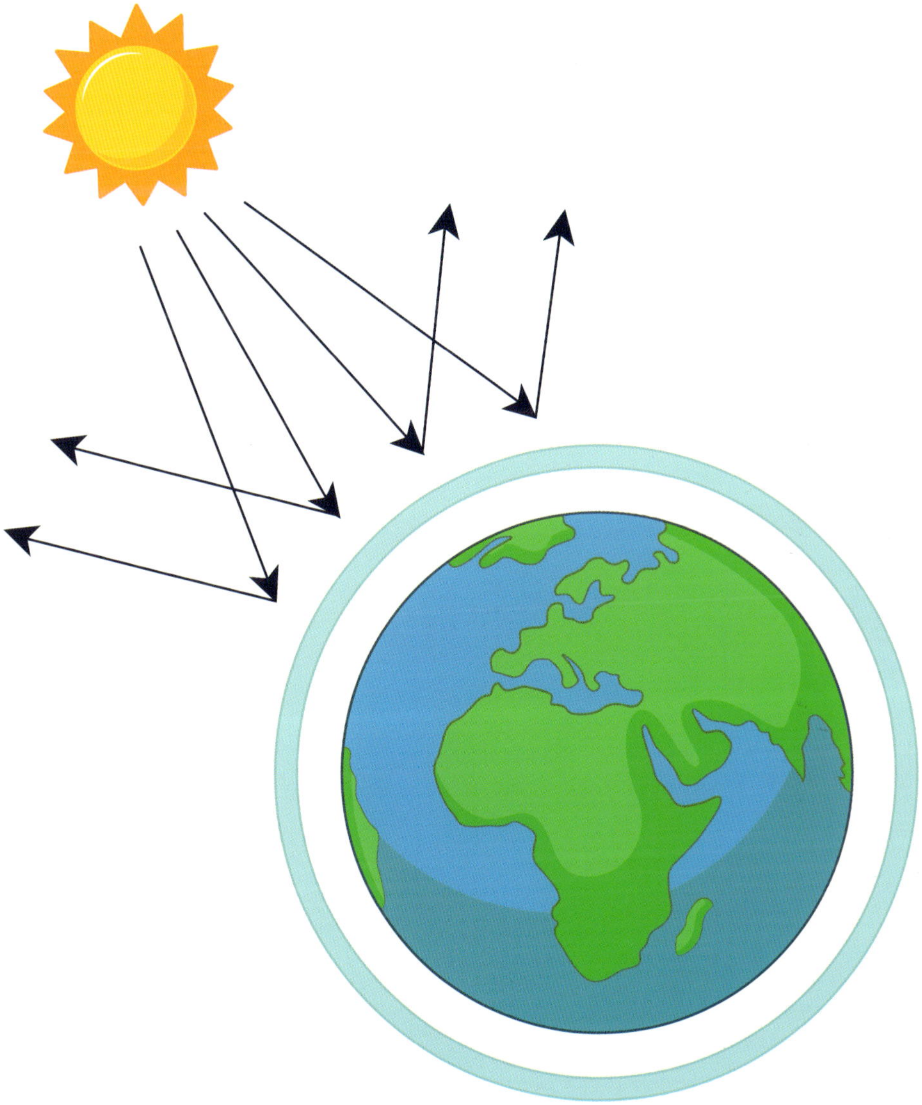

P Pollution

The release of unwanted substances into the environment

Q

Quarry

A large, deep pit where stone
or other materials are
removed from

R

Recycle

To turn waste into new things

S Solar Power

The use of the sun to obtain energy

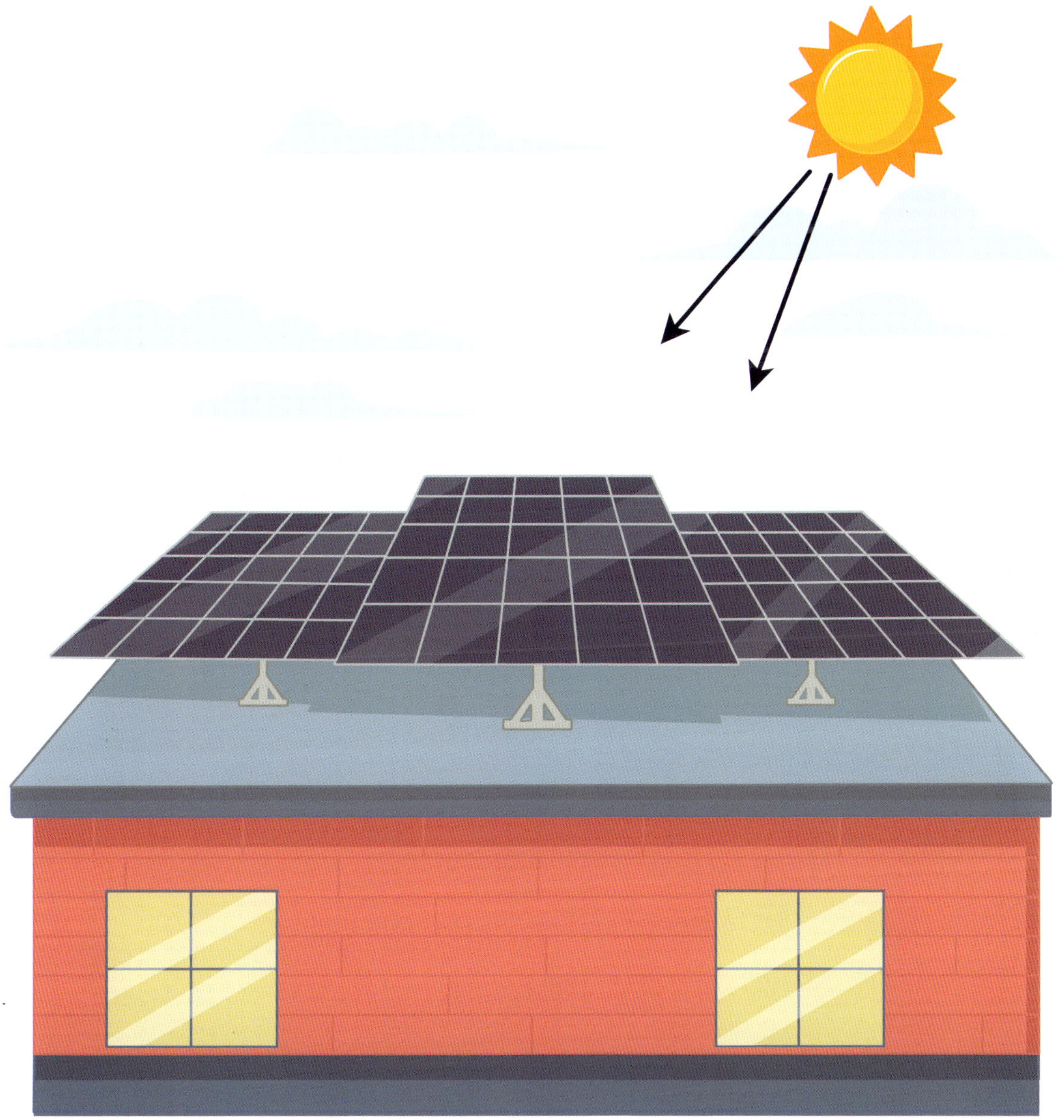

T

Toxic

Poisonous or harmful to the body

U

Urban Runoff

Rainwater that drains from city streets

V

Vapour

Gas or tiny drops of liquid that result from heating a liquid or solid

W

Watershed

An area of land that drains water into a waterbody

X

Xerophyte

A plant that survives where there is little water

Y

Yard Waste

This is made of grass clippings, dead plants, sticks, branches and leaves

Z Zooplankton

Tiny animals that live in water

Pick up recyclables as you make your way to the bin

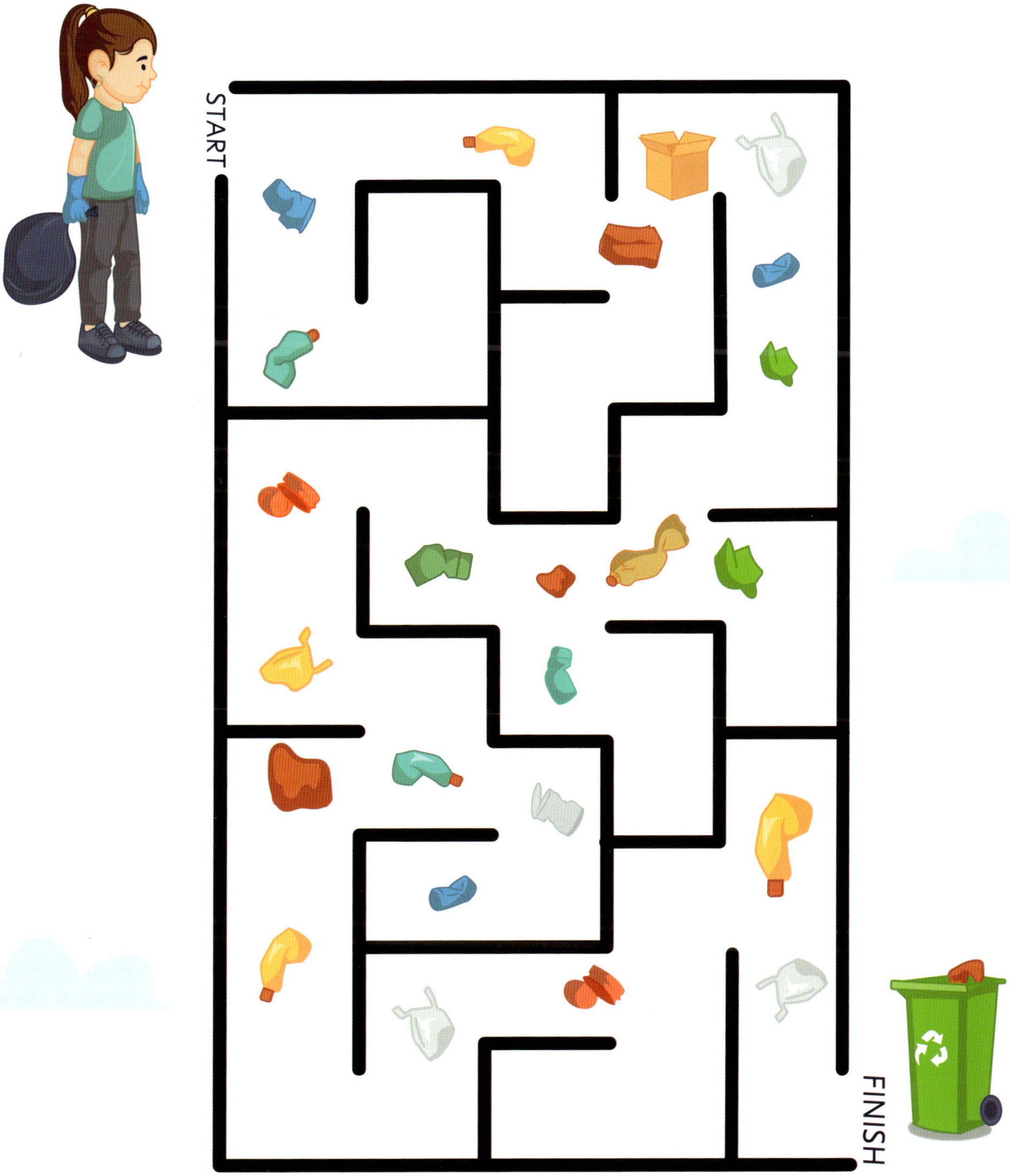

Match the word to the picture

Zooplankton

Ozone layer

Toxic

Solar power

Recycle

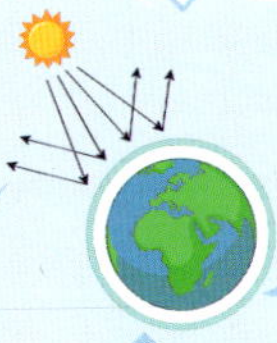